# HOT DROP

## J DARK

Cover artwork © 2017 by Niki Lenhart
*nikilen-designs.com*

Published by Paper Angel Press
*paperangelpress.com*

ISBN 978-1-944412-81-4 (Trade Paperback)

10 9 8 7 6 5 4 3 2

## Acknowledgments

*Thank you to Paper Angel Press,
for all the editing and the printing of this slim volume.
Thanks to the Saturday and Sunday gang,
for input and suggestions,
and a big thank you
to all the readers who encourage writers
to go above and beyond to write good stories.*

## Dedication

*This is for all you readers:
Thank you for having a look at this story.
It's your imagination, curiosity and joy of reading that make
stories like this possible.
You may never know how much writers appreciate their
readers, but I hope this gives you a hint of how much we
enjoy your reading habit and especially your feedback,
both positive and negative.
Without your input, we'd never know how much you like
reading, so, once again, thank you so much for reading,
and please send your opinions to us.
We'd love to hear from you!*

# Hot Drop

T HE HATCHWAY DOOR SWUNG OPEN, slamming with a hollow clang against the bulkhead. The lanky Sergeant Vinson, in full combat gear, woke the team. His raspy drawl sounded like a bandsaw cutting metal.

"Y'all be gettin' up! Control's got us'ns a mission ta go! Report fer briefin' in five!"

"Yes, Sergeant!" The six-unit team shouted as they scrambled out of their bunks and stumbled to their lockers.

Corporal Tripoli watched the others beginning their daily kit up. Grabbing the door of her locker, she lifted its latch. Its door swung open, revealing her gray jumpsuit uniform, fittable armor plates, and wrap-around torso armor with its air-tight helmet. She pulled her helmet on and checked the seals. Satisfied, she removed the helmet and hung it back on its peg. Next, she grabbed her jumpsuit and zipped in. She finished kitting up, then pulled the helmet back out of the locker, hanging it on a belt loop before hurrying after the others to the briefing.

The briefing room aboard the *Erie* was a small alcove set along inside bulkhead of the bridge. At the center of the floor, a small holotable was already active. There was just enough room for the troopers to squeeze around it.

Lieutenant Kestrel waved his hand over the table, then gestured upward. A blue and green sphere rose from the table, then stopped to hover at eye level, spinning slowly. Normally, there would be more colors on the map, depicting terrain features like deserts and mountain ranges. Here, there was only green and blue, vegetation and water. The unrelieved green was confusing, as if the data was incomplete.

"You'll note," the Lieutenant said firmly, "that there's only two forms of terrain: forest, and water." He paused a moment. "The forest consists of the same vegetation throughout its reach; the screen isn't broken. Every piece of land above water is covered by vegetation."

The ethereal orb continued to rotate, showing the distributions of land and water. A single yellow spot blinked on the southernmost landmass. Kestrel clicked a button. The hologram flattened and zoomed in dizzyingly to reveal rugged terrain and the outline of a three-building complex. Seven red spots appeared on the screen.

"This is your objective." A red dot appeared south of the objective. Kestrel continued, "This is your insertion point. They'll know you're coming. We can't get into position in stealth mode because of the defense screen. You will make a low-orbit drop by rocket-assist capsule, and deploy at three hundred meters above the ground." He paused, scanning the alert faces around the table. "The landing's going to be rough; I won't lie. You're going to have minimal time to control the drop. Blip the brakes fast, get to ground, and off enemy radar."

Kestrel frowned, then continued. "We don't know what kind of anti-air defenses are deployed. One thing's certain: with a defense screen that sophisticated out here, this place is going to have equally sophisticated weaponry to repel attacks. Keep your heads low, listen to your squad leaders ... and Take. That. Objective. Get the job done, and come home. Good luck. Prepare for drop."

"YESSIR!"

The team jogged in formation to drop fitting. The suits they wore consisted of a series of exoskeletons that surrounded the operator. Armor was eventually added, contoured to roughly fit a humanoid outline. The armor bulged around the active frame, making the suit appear vaguely gorilla-like, with large, thick arms and legs in contrast to the relatively thin torso that housed the trooper. Each suit was modified according to the wearer from its standard design.

Vinson led the team past Wendell's suit, which towered over them. He was the heavy support. The suit was reinforced, its skeleton laminated to handle the auto-cannon's recoil. Wendell's armor was easily a head taller than all the others, reaching three and a half meters. Wendell himself was about as opposite as possible from the imposing suit he operated. Quiet and almost invisible, even in groups, he never stood out, even with his eye-catching two-meter height.

Marco's suit was next. His suit was heavily customized. The tiger-striped black and brown wasn't regulation, but Marco was very good, and Command cut him some slack as the pattern wasn't neon orange and yellow, like a previous time. Vinson shook his head. He'd never met anyone who wanted attention like Marco. The man would wear a clown suit on a battlefield. Despite the extreme extroversion, Marco *was* a team player *par excellence.* He'd never pulled anything that threatened unit integrity while on-mission. Off-mission was another matter, and not something the sergeant worried about.

As Marco dropped out of line to suit up, he passed the smallest suit. Barely the minimum one-point-seven meters tall, Carter's suit seemed even smaller cradling the Mk-951 assault weapon. Carter had passed as "Expert" in the weapon, and was a sniper-quality marksman. He was, like his suit, small, intense, and focused. Just slightly over a meter and a half tall. Pale-skinned and very lean, he looked almost emaciated. He'd shaved his head and lathered down with chemical epilators so that his suit contacts and feedback had no hair that might cause even a blip of resistance. Vinson wondered at this, as the sensors had no trouble with hair, but Carter had insisted. Carter's quirks weren't troublesome to the team on mission, so Vinson let it slide.

The next suit had curves no man could fit into. This was Tripoli, Vinson's assistant squad leader. Like her namesake, she was dark-haired, brown-eyed, and olive-skinned. She also stood just over a meter and a half tall, and could handle a Mk-951 like a kid's plastic toy. Like the others, she had her quirks, but those quirks had kept her and others in her squad alive. Her focus on mission was laser tight. It made her a good number two, but Vinson didn't think she'd make squad leader until she got more flexible in her thinking. Like the others, her ability to hyper-focus was both a weakness and a strength.

Last came Simon. His suit was so regulation that it seemed out of order. It was the only suit the sergeant had ever seen that did not have some kind of modification. It matched its wearer to a "T". Of the team, Simon was the most laconic out of mission. He was also the most even-tempered in mission as well. His laid-back demeanor was nearly alien to Vinson and the others. Vinson hated his attitude, but loved his skills. Simon himself was just a shade over one and a half meters, and massed one hundred thirty kilograms. Stocky, but with unbelievable endurance, he was the team's medical specialist. His skills were called upon when the armor could not control a wound — which was, fortunately, not often.

Vinson marched to his suit and saluted it. It had earned that respect from him. His suit looked battered, and almost slovenly, but Vinson wouldn't have it look any other way. Each hole was patched, but not cleaned and smoothed. The dents from shrapnel were left untouched, just the paint replaced. Each time he looked at the suit, he counted each mortal wound it had saved him from. To date, the count was twenty-seven; he'd be dead that many times without it. He dropped the heartfelt salute, stepped onto the small platform, did a precise about-face, and stepped backward into the suit, which started through the automatic button-up sequence.

Once sealed and cycled, the team marched down the gantry to the drop chutes. Vinson had them count off by numbers and step to each opening. The platforms dropped them to loading, where their armor activated, drawing the soldiers up into fetal positions, then enclosed each of them in a gleaming, finned egg.

The ship bucked as it skimmed the top of the atmosphere. Readouts in the capsules reported their oxygen use, blood energy, and administered drugs to ease those whose heart rates went above the physiological optimum.

Weapons reported ready, and the spatial coordinates fed into the capsules, aiming them at their targets. Wendell, the auto-cannon support member, began to hum off-key. The tune was picked up by Simon, who, unlike Wendell, had an ear for music.

The two dissonant warbles grated on Tripoli's nerves. "Shut up or there's gonna be friendly fire!" she growled into the comm.

"Easy Corp," said Wendell. "We'll take it private."

Two light pops indicated that the two men had left the channel to private A, just as an extra strong buffet gave notice that the drop units were unshackled and primed for launch. There was barely enough time for the troopers to take a breath when the rockets engaged and the seals popped, using the air in the tube as the propelling charge. The fins shifted, jinking the capsule in random directions to throw off any enemy targeting. The troopers didn't feel the ride, as neural white noise was fed into their nervous systems, essentially putting them into a state of total sensory deprivation.

The missiles jinked again, and then accelerated toward the surface. Their outside surface temperature climbed to eleven hundred degrees Celsius from the atmospheric friction. After thirty seconds of no hostile response, the capsules straightened their trajectory, and powered down toward the target zone.

Two long minutes passed for Lieutenant Kestrel as he watched the individual capsules streak toward the ground. The systems reported optimum zones for all of his charges. Smiling grimly as his men dropped, he activated the link, then sent a test pulse to check for any jamming. When he got the signal back, Kestrel boosted the signal and set the scrambler to active. The computer would analyze the jamming and look for weaker signal strength to punch through, or open frequencies to operate within the white noise. On the ground, the same kind of electronic war was being waged, trying to identify the intruders, and estimating their landing trajectories.

The neural link dropped. Carter came awake immediately, the warning pings of capsule breakup were sounding, readying him to blip the boot jets to start arresting his fall. He had enough extra fuel for twenty seconds of burn; three seconds would halt a terminal dive. His computer was giving him a choice of controlled burn, fast drop, or manual.

He blinked at the manual control on his HUD, then yelled "Hands in the air, riders!", before laughing with the adrenalin rush and blipping his boot jets.

Kestrel saw Carter, Vinson, and Marco drop computer control for manual, and smiled for a moment. "You wreck those suits, you Yahoos, you're doing latrine duty for the next twenty years."

His eyes were drawn to the screens as the boat's optics detected movement on the ground at the base. "Our hosts are rolling out a hot welcome. No heavy weapons identified, yet. Twelve count, no armor. IR says the weapons are warm, lasers or plasma tech, most likely. We've got twenty laser bursts, should you need 'em."

"Loud and clear, mother hen," Tripoli said over the comm. "You get a call if we need you to lay an egg."

A couple of muffled laughs came over the comm. The lieutenant smiled then said, "Ten seconds to touchdown, you're armed, weapons hot, HUD link on. Hoooah!"

"HOOAH!"

The capsules burst, their pieces darting away under power, broadcasting random signals to draw fire away from the dropping marines.

•       •       •

The drop went totally uncontested. No anti-drop fire. No missiles. Nothing. As the squad dropped, boot jets fired asymmetrically in programmed jinks and jukes, creating random shifts in direction and speed to foil targeting. They dropped into the trees. Its canopy swallowed them, forcing the light compensators to adjust rapidly, making the interior of their helmets seem to flicker. Once down, the drones were launched, two per squaddie. Each drone fed data of the surrounding terrain, heat signatures, air samples, and medical information to the orbiting mother ship. The drones, about the size and shape of a thumb, skittered back and forth on small, motor-less fans set at their corners, allowing them to hover silently and change direction in an eye blink. The drones swiftly dispersed, according to squaddie tactical assignment.

The humidity measured in the low ninety percent, with the atmospheric temperature a sweltering 40 degrees Celsius. The leaves overhead were so thick, light barely penetrated to the forest floor. On the ground, the closest thing Vinson could compare the visibility to was a deep twilight. All the trunks and branches seemed to almost melt into one another in the near-darkness.

Rotting vegetation covered with the forest floor. Nothing grew the first six meters up; there just wasn't enough sunlight. The middle canopy was a ten-meter-thick crazy quilt of moss, dead branches, and vines. The top canopy was about four meters thick, with entwined branches sprouting what looked like leaves of every shape and color imaginable.

The highest leaves were every shade of green, with brighter hues lower into the canopy. Green gave way to yellows, then oranges and reds as the light dimmed. Under the suits' lights, blue feathery things shared space with orange clusters and reddish branches that seemed to create a net at the base of the upper sections. The light breeze that moved the upper leaves seemed to transmit its way down to the lower areas, where even the small patches of moss swayed in time with the upper branches, although there seemed to be no discernible wind to move them.

Most striking, the sergeant noted, was the absence of noise: no buzzing insects, no wildlife calls — just the quiet rustling of leaves overhead, and the soft, woody creak of swaying branches. The silence was so encompassing that it seemed press down and cover everything like a shroud.

The marines unlimbered their pulse rifles and swiftly moved to assigned locations. Alert and ready for a fight, they dug in, their armored hands tearing scars in the earth to lie down in. Entrenched and camouflaged, they waited for the enemy counterattack they knew was coming.

"You think they're gonna come on the ground or in the trees, Wendy?" Carter whispered over the comm.

"Twenty cred on a ground attack," replied Wendell, with a muffled grunt that might have been a laugh.

"Shet. Hell. Up." said Vinson. The authority in his voice cut through all chatter, leaving the channel dead.

"Attention squad one-two-two, you have movement your direction. Mother counts seven — confirm seven — with contact. One-two click, twice to acknowledge." Simon keyed his mic twice, the double click registered by the ship. The code made hacked communications more certain. Calling the member number with the request made it hard for the hacker to duplicate quickly.

"Team tuh, up thet ridge, low on our'n sahide. Make shor y'all got good covah", Vinson ordered.

"On it," Tripoli replied. "Marco, you're point. Wendell, you're drag. Move out."

Marco grunted over the comm, then sent his two drones ahead to sweep for hostiles and map terrain. Tripoli did the same directly over the team, with Wendell running sweep circuits at the rear.

"Sahmon, oveah thar, Cartah, over thar. A'll be up front fuhst. Use hand signals heah on out. Make shor ya got cover fiah for us'n if we need it."

Both men nodded and melted into the dark, their combat armor displayed matching background patterns as they moved, rendering them nearly invisible to human eyes.

Vinson thought for a moment, then dialed up the low light option for his armor. As dark as this place was, there'd likely be some sharp eyes in the forest. He checked the ammo counter on the clip, then brushed his hand across his web-belt, making certain everything was in place. His fingers touched the small, sewn-on snap pouch just to the left of the buckle, hapatics in the suit letting him feel the small imperfections in its stitching. The pouch wasn't regulation, but, for him, was his strongest reason for service. His fingers stroked the pouch tenderly, then dropped to the pistol grip of the pulse rifle. He bent his arm overhead, straightened it twice, and then started working slowly along the ridge.

The going was rapid., With little undergrowth to traverse, they moved the first five kilometers quickly. The drones kept reporting no movement, no local wildlife. The last was very unusual. Every place had some kind of indigenous life.

Tripoli and her team checked in visually, making certain no one was drifting out of formation as they paralleled Vinson's team. Everything they saw was the same: absolutely no animal life of any kind, the branches and leaves moving as if pushed by a light breeze. All of the instruments in their suits recorded no air movement strong enough to account for their motion. The wet ground muffled their steps, making their reconnaissance absolutely silent, except for the odd moment when a suit would brush against a trunk or a low-hanging branch. It created an eerie, unsettling feeling as the team approached the structure that the lieutenant had highlighted.

"Hell! What happened to my drones?!" Carter's voice cut across the comm like a knife.

"SHET UP, CARTER!" Vinson roared.

Marco checked his drones "vitals". They all showed green, then nothing. Simon watched the same thing happen. No red blinking lights for a malfunction, no beeping indicating a target lock on the drone. Just there, then gone.

Vinson guessed the drones were being taken out by their yet-unseen enemy. Just how they were doing it, was the question. The last of the drones winked out, leaving them dependent on their own suits and senses.

Using hand signals, Vinson slowed the squad's approach. Moving slower was the only tactic to deal with the loss of the drones. They still hadn't seen anything of their supposed enemy after the first contact back on the ship. The six marines moved carefully over the top of the ridge, and then partway down the sunward side. The objective of the recon and rescue lay before them.

The structure was massive. Vinson pulled out his binoculars and dialed back the power to fit it all within his sight picture, then keyed the binoculars to measure the distance. Data flashed across the display:

RANGE:1.411KM WIDTH: 2.103 KM HEIGHT: .608KM

Vinson pulled the binoculars down.

*Christamighty, it's huge. The trees must be twice, three times the size of what we've seen so far. Where are the hostiles the ship showed us? This place is dead quiet.*

Vinson raised his hand, then clenched it twice. The two fire teams hunkered down and set up covering fire.

•      •      •

Simon moved into a small clearing, away from the cover of the trees. He unlimbered his entrenching tool and rapidly dug a shallow pit to lie in. He didn't know why, but being near those softly swaying branches sent shivers up his spine. A few moments later, he was in the trench with his rifle propped up on a small berm of soil. From his position, he could easily cover Vinson's path along the edge of the structure.

*The sooner I'm offa this rock, the better. Place reminds me of a cemetery; nothing but breeze in the leaves. Wonder where all the wildlife is? A place like this ought to have at least some kind of local bugs.*

He shook his head then lowered his eye to the 'scope once more.

Vinson continued his slow traverse along the edge of the vegetation. He watched the Sarge for a few more paces, then swept ahead and behind, looking for any movement. When he swept back to check Vinson, he saw the Sarge step behind some brush. He never came out.

Simon waited for a few moments, then swept his scope back and forth, checking for any movement. He scanned the opposite slope, ground, everything, three times before he decided to move out toward the Sarge's last visible position. He hand-signaled the corporal, then moved out, fighting his revulsion as he stuck to the darkest, densest cover he could find. Slowly, he picked his way down slope toward the last location where he had seen the sergeant.

"Private Simon, do you have eyes on Sergeant Vinson? We've lost telemetry from the squad leader. Signals are flatline." After the enforced silence, the corporal's voice sounded like an explosion in his ear. Simon dropped to one knee, looking about carefully from his limited vantage point in the huge trees. There was nothing — only the slightly swaying leaves and branches that they had trekked through. He tapped his comm twice for a negative reply.

"This is Lieutenant Harris. Corporal Tripoli, until Sergeant Vincent's status is ascertained, you are acting squad leader. Radio silence is hereby revoked. Members, call in by the numbers."

"One-two. One-three. Two-one. Two-two. Two-three," the members called in.

"We copy, sir. Permission to speak, sir?" Tripoli said.

"Granted," Harris agreed.

"Why break silence now?" Tripoli asked bluntly.

She looked around at the others, and saw the same question in their eyes. Breaking comm silence was not something the team did, or the commander did, during ops. This change in operations surprised everyone.

"Your team is compromised, Corporal. Sergeant Vinson disappeared without a trace. What is your assessment of your situation? Is operational silence going to be any advantage?"

Tripoli considered this for a moment. "No. If the Sarge's been taken by locals, silence isn't going to help us. They'll have been tracking us for a while to take Vinson so fast."

"Command agrees. If we had not been observing operational silence, we may have had warning, and been able to direct you beforehand," Harris said. "We still need the structure scouted. That is your first priority. Second is Sergeant Vinson. Mark his last known location. Recon and return here. Command will scan from here and see if we can locate the sergeant. Questions, Corporal?"

"None, sir. Repeating orders: recon structure, find sergeant Vincent, rendezvous after recon this location."

"Correct. Move out, and good luck."

Tripoli looked at the team. "You heard Command. We've got recon to do."

"Yes, Corporal," they said in unison.

"One team, Simon, you're point. Wendell, you're drag. Carter, you're moving with Simon. Marco with Wendell. We go bounding overwatch. We're going to move one and a half klicks North, then turn and go in from the Northwest. This place is big; don't get confused by the size. Gear on. Simon, you and Carter are go."

●　　　●　　　●

Tripoli watched the two marines moved North. They ran three seconds hard, then dropped, rolling in opposite directions, stopping when they were behind cover. She nodded to Wendell, and he and Marco moved out, with Tripoli dropping next to Simon. She watched them rush past Simon and Carter, then run a good twenty meters past, and then drop, rolling and seeking cover. Then she was up with Simon and Carter, stopping next to Wendell as they rushed up.

They kept up the grueling pace for the next thirty minutes, each team advancing by ten to twenty meters. No one said anything, alert for any motion not their own. Their movements were fast, compact, running low to avoid stirring any branches, their feet picking up cleanly to avoid shuffling and noise. Each fall, controlled, being a half-roll to deaden the impact and present the most difficult moving target. With all the care and attention they paid, only the stuttering sounds of their own footfalls could be heard. The absolute silence wore on Tripoli; she knew it wore on the others, too.

*What kind of place is this?* Tripoli wondered silently, growing more concerned about the Sarge's disappearance.

When her inertial compass reported that they'd moved a half-kilometer past the north edge of the huge edifice, she called a halt. All of the marines were breathing hard, almost exhausted by their pace and actions.

"Water and food, no fire, make it fast. The hard part comes next," she told her team.

As they ate and rested up, she moved to the crest of the ridge and tried to look down at the structure through the trees. She knew where the structure was, according to the downloaded map in her wrist comp, but it proved impossible to see from her vantage point.

*We'll take it slower now, and a* lot *tighter.*

Tripoli watched the huge trees in the distance sway rhythmically back and forth. Even with her external laser microphones turned up as sensitive as possible, there was no sound. No wind. No creak of swaying trees. Only total silence — except for her team's voices and her own breathing. The silence felt ominous, and somehow alive. Her thoughts made her shiver.

*Why can't I shake this feeling? It's like we're whistling in a cemetery.*

"Command, reporting no hostiles. What happened to the seven signals during the drop?" she inquired.

The silence over the comm seemed to stretch out for minutes.

"We don't know," Command finally replied.

"What do you mean, you don't know, sir?" Tripoli demanded, seething inwardly.

*How can you not KNOW what happened to seven hostiles? We had satellites launched. We have full coverage of the area! How did you fucking LOSE seven hostiles?*

"Control's best guess is stealth technology. We're working that angle, and hope to re-establish contact soon." There was a pause, then Command said, "Parameters remain the same. You have a schedule to keep, Corporal. We will keep you updated."

"Updated, hell! You find them! I'm tired of being led by the nose in a place that doesn't have anything we're looking for, and you damn well haven't said anything about this 'science expedition' that we're supposed to find! What in HELL are we doing here?"

•       •       •

She made certain the channel remained private. Sealing herself in, and turning her ECM systems fully active, she raged at their nebulous orders. It was clear to her that the entire mission had been a misdirection of some kind, but for her life she couldn't figure out why. There seemed to be no reason for the sudden capriciousness of their orders. As she raged inwardly, it felt like a fog was lifting. Her head started to ache, then cleared.

*What the hell is happening?*

She remembered the mission. They'd been tasked with a rescue, to be certain, but it was a rescue of the rescue team and the original science team.

"Our last mission was a complete failure. Something affected the team through the power suits. There was no communication and the radio chatter, while sounding normal, was not the parameters that had been in the briefing. Keep alert and observe two changes in standard operational procedures. One, always remain in visual range of each other. Do not use your HUD; use your eyes. Two, maintain constant communications with Control. Keep the comm open at all times. Do not go dark."

*We blew it! What is going on here? How did … the ECM gear. I turned it on to keep from being heard by Control.*

Tripoli looked at the others, all of whom had settled down on the damp earth. Their bodies had turned toward her, waiting for orders.

She moved to the nearest soldier, and pressed her helmet to his. "Wendell, can you hear me?"

"Shore can, Corp."

"Turn on your ECM, then get Marco to turn his on."

"Done." Wendell's hands came up to his helmet. "Oh man!" He started to pull at his helmet, then stopped.

Tripoli kept her helmet tight against his. "Wendell, you good?"

"Frosty, Corp. What is that? My gawd, what they hell was hap'nin to us?"

"Get over to Marco, and get him on ECM. I'll get Simon and Carter."

A few minutes later, all five had their ECM on and were discussing the situation. They huddled close, five helmets in a circle pressed tight to one another, so their voices could be heard.

"We call for pickup, and get this intel back to Control," Marco said.

"No. In order to call for pickup, we have to drop the ECM, and we don't know how fast this operates. For all we know, it could be instant," Tripoli said tersely.

"They gotta know something's up. Going dark was what they specifically said not to do," Simon replied, remembering their orders.

"Good sense," Tripoli replied. "But the wrong choice here. ECM's the only thing that cleared our heads."

"I wonder why it works," Simon asked thoughtfully.

"Right now, I don't care. It's got our heads clear, so we keep them going and see about the Sarge first, then the mission," Tripoli said. "You apes ready to go?"

"Locked and loaded!" came four muffled voices.

"Good. Simon, Carter. First team, you lead out. We go a slow walk. Watch for movement or noise. Use hand signals. If you see something, call huddle."

"Yes, Corp," both Simon and Carter replied.

"Move out." Tripoli told them.

•　　•　　•

Now that their minds were clear again, the soldiers noticed much more around them. The forest seemed alive, watching them as they backtracked to Vincent's last location. They found him within ten feet of his last transponder location. His suit was partly covered with what appeared to be roots. His armor had been etched and weakened by what seemed to be a viscous acid seeping from the roots. The team converged to pull at the roots and try to tear them away from the sergeant. Wendell checked Vincent's armor over carefully, while Simon checked his bio readings.

"The etching's bad. Another hour or so, and the roots would have breached the armor," Wendell informed Tripoli. "It's barely airtight right now. He needs repairs."

"He needs emergency evac, and we can't do it," Tripoli replied. "Simon, can you get the suit to pump him with stimulants? We need him alert."

"I don't think it's gonna help, Corp. These readings say he's in a coma. The stimulants will just boost his heart, not wake him," Simon said. "He needs a full medical."

Tripoli growled in frustration. She looked around at the faces in the helmets. Her command. Her responsibility.

"Simon, you carry the Sarge. I'll take point. We go slow. Move out."

•     •     •

The team moved slowly back down into the bowl. The silence they first encountered was still absolute, but now the movement of the plants felt all had more ominous. Grass, brush, and tree limbs all seemed to stretch toward them as they passed. Everyone in the team seemed disturbed by this, Tripoli observed. The helmets would turn and focus on each movement until the troopers stepped past it, and then their helmets would swivel to the next large movement.

Simon was especially agitated as he tried to make certain he was facing the threat. Sarge was his responsibility, and nothing was going to get to his charge while he lived. The trees continued to grow larger as they descended to the bottom of the bowl, becoming as big around as some of the pictures of the extinct sequoias on Earth. To look at them was to feel dwarfed by their magnitude.

They moved slowly toward the stone structure. Compared to the ancient solidity of the trees, the buildings seemed an aberration. No visible impressions of their age were immediately apparent. Their surface seemed fresh and new. Up close, Tripoli couldn't see any visible lines where blocks nestled against each other to form the walls of the structure. The wall itself was forty meters tall, and stretched for a half-kilometer. Its single doorway looked like a small mouse hole by comparison.

The team moved into position, with Carter and Wendell flanking the doorway. Tripoli waved them over, and the team again leaned into a huddle, helmets touching.

"It's the only place we can go, and I already hate it," she told them. "Carter, you're point. Wendell, you're drag. We're likely gonna be single file in there. Simon's in the middle. I'll be behind Carter. Marco will be behind Simon. Keep the jammers going and keep your eyes open." She checked her chronometer. "Thirty seconds to check weapons, then we go."

"Yes, Corporal!" came the reply.

Carter took two deep breaths, clicked on his helmet light, and then the camera. He rolled around the corner, his weapon raised. The light beaming from his helmet showed a narrow corridor going straight for at least eighty meters, which was the limit of its range. He switched to infrared to see if there was a difference and, when no detail emerged, returned to standard light.

The five marines slowly moved down the narrow, cramped corridor. Compared to outside, this was nowhere near as threatening. Close-quarters and house-to-house combat they were trained for; for a silent, enigmatic forest that seemed alive, they weren't.

Ten minutes later, the corridor expanded into a large cavern. As the moved into the immense space, the air seemed to begin to glow with pale bluish-green light. A few more steps into the cavern brought the light up to a normal daylight level.

The place was enormous. The ceiling registered on sonic ranging as two hundred meters overhead. The room measured as three hundred meters across, and nearly the same wide. A soft material covered the floor. The database reported it to be a fungus.

The five marines had moved together to huddle and discuss options, when Vincent went into cardiac arrest. His suit began beeping loudly. Simon rolled the sergeant onto his back and plugged into its emergency override circuit. Rapidly, he scanned the physiological readings, which were all red-lined.

Vincent's heart was pushing two hundred forty beats a minute; oxygen saturation was down to a bare minimum.

Blood pressure, even with the high heart rate, was barely eighty over fifty, and sinking fast. Diagnostics indicated critical nerve damage. Simon looked on in helpless agony as Sarge's heart suddenly seized, and then stilled.

Tripoli leaned her helmet against Simon's. "How bad is he?"

"Gone, he's gone. We can't even suspend him. There's no way the suit could take the temperature, damaged like it is."

Even as he spoke, Simon was keying the emergency cryogenic response in Vincent's suit. The system began to hum. Micro-lasers fired, cooling the suit, and Vincent's body, for cryogenic suspension. The suit beeped a warning as stress on it increased from the temperature gradient. There came a slight groaning sound, then the weakened ceramic gave way with a sharp crack, crumbling into pieces. The laser array shorted as the electrical storage discharged with a loud pop and a bright blue spark.

"You tried," Tripoli said, with forced, focused calm. "Wrap him and set him by the tunnel. We'll pick him up on the way out."

The group was somber as they wrapped the sergeant in an environmental blanket. A quick spray of adhesive sealed the covering. Once the sergeant's remains were positioned by the door, Tripoli called them all to a huddle.

"Whatever's going on, we're seeing this through. Sarge would want it that way. Simon, you're point. Wendell, you're second. Marco, drag. Carter, behind me. Whatever's down here is what we're after, and we're gonna get it." Tripoli paused, then said sharply. "Move out!"

"Yes, Corp!"

●　　　●　　　●

The team shouldered their weapons, and started slowly across the floor in single file. Each marine was careful to follow the foot prints of the squaddie in front, hoping to avoid any weaknesses or traps hidden in the soft fungus floor. Simon slowly worked his way across the cavern, angling left, toward the only other opening he could see. As they approached the archway, it became clear that this was an artificially enlarged passage. The corridor was much too clean, much too regular, to be natural.

*This is the real deal now*, thought Tripoli.

She checked her safety by flicking it on and off, making certain her weapon was ready. The others checked their weapons. This change meant that the mission was on now. With a heightened sense of purpose, the small group pushed forward down the corridor.

The darkness began to fade as they moved down the narrow passageway. Light seemed to come from all around them: the floor, walls, and ceiling.

*I wonder if it's piezoelectric?* Simon wondered.

He increased his pace slightly to move ahead of the others a few extra meters. The others widened the gap between themselves also, taking the cue from Simon. If any blast happened, spreading out lessened the chance of all of them getting taken out at once.

The light continued to increase as they moved, becoming so bright that the soldiers had to deploy their sun filters to see at all. Tripoli tapped Wendell on the shoulder, then motioned for him to tap Simon and stop. She wanted to see if the light would fade when they quit moving.

Tripoli motioned them over and got them in a helmet-to-helmet huddle once more.

"What we have is a lotta light from somewhere." She checked her readouts, which irritatingly showed no unusual energy or magnetic readings.

*This is really giving me a bad feeling. There should be some kind of energy spike to get light like this, but the suit's sensors say nothing's there.*

She gritted her teeth for a moment, then took a deep breath to calm herself before speaking again. "I think it might be from us, charging something as we walk. We're going to take a fifteen-minute break to see if the light dissipates." She looked around the huddle at the darkened helmets.

"What iffen it don' disa whattis?" said someone.

*Carter*, Tripoli thought from the accent. "Then we improvise," she replied, "and keep going. This is the only path, so it's the only way the science team and the other rescue parties could have gone."

"What do you think the others did with the light?" another muffled voice asked.

"Probably the same we're gonna do: live with it ... if we have to," Tripoli said as an answer. She didn't like the idea of going into the light.

The glaring brightness held its intensity for five minutes, then began to fade slowly. As the soldiers waited for the light to weaken completely, they re-checked their weapons, re-checked their suits, and re-checked their ECM gear, making certain everything was ready.

It took another fifteen minutes for the light to disappear entirely. Oddly, their suits didn't register any brightness change. Tripoli had to manually flip on her helmet light on in order to see.

*I wonder if they waited like that?,* Tripoli asked herself.

Units like hers were trained for aggressive action and, usually, any obstacle was met and dealt with through improvisation. "Be a smart marine. Figger it owt on th' flahy," Vincent had told them time and again during practice. Tripoli thought about the words, and wondered about the first rescue team.

*I don't think they did slow down for the light. It might have done them.*

Her helmet light revealed the long narrow corridor once more. As they moved down the passageway, the floor was barely illuminated with a faint-bluish green tinge. Tripoli took point this time, checking her weapon to find it charged and the safety off. She carried it low in both hands. Each step had her swiveling her head forward, up, left, and right, checking everything in front of her for any hints of traps or irregularities in the floor or walls.

The light slowly strengthened again as they pressed forward. This time, it increased to a particular level and stayed there, right near normal daylight. The effect was somewhat disorienting, as the light radiated from underfoot.

Another ten minutes brought them to another widening in the tunnel. The huge, nearly spherical cavern stretched for nearly eight hundred meters across, according to Tripoli's ranging optics. The narrow footpath angled down into the depressed center, where a large nest of strange objects sat. The entire area covered by the objects stretched two hundred meters across the floor of the sphere, creating a maze the team would have to travel through to get to the other side.

Simon kneeled at the sharp edge of the bowl and ran a finger along its smooth surface. "We don't want to go that way. It feels like it's greased."

"Dafihn greezed, Simon," Wendell asked him.

"We get a free ride to the bottom. I don't know if we could stand up once we got there. My fingers couldn't get the slightest grip when I tried to check how smooth it is," Simon reported quietly.

Tripoli looked at the faintly-lit path angling down to the machines. She motioned the team to huddle and touch helmets again.

"Stay on the path, weapons hot. That looks like too good a place for an ambush," she growled at them.

"Yes, Corp!"

"Look for anything that might give us a clue where that first rescue team and the scientists are. Rescue is first priority, after staying alive to do it."

"Yes, Corp!"

"I've got lead. Wendell, you're number two. Simon, you've got rear. Carter, you've got left; Marco right. Six meters between. We can't jump off the path, so keep the distance."

She straightened up without waiting for the reply, checked the ammo counter on her rifle, then started slowly down the narrow walkway. Once she'd gone seven steps, Wendell moved onto the path, his weapon aimed down, ready to fire, his finger resting lightly across the trigger guard. Each member started seven steps behind the previous squaddie, with Simon following last.

Their sense of proportion seemed all out of place once they started in. The "towers" seemed to enlarge oddly as the team moved closer, looming over the marines like antediluvian monsters of stone. Strange machinery spun and blinked as they stepped to the edge of the first tower. Tripoli's range finder reported the distance across its base as three hundred meters. Perplexed, she measured the range again and got the same result.

"How can the bowl be eight hundred across, and just one of these things be three hundred alone?" she muttered to herself.

Tripoli checked to make certain her suit was sealed. A strange reading like this might mean she was falling under the influence of whatever was in the atmosphere again. When the integrity check showed a green light, she shouldered her weapon and slowly moved in between the weird objects.

Gravity here fluctuated constantly. One moment, the pull would be normal. Then, in the distance of a few steps, it would swing, and the team would find itself angling up to twenty degrees from vertical, forcing the marines to gyrate wildly to stay upright. Another few steps, and they'd stagger under twice the pull what they were used to, then a few steps later, scrambling frantically as they suddenly weighed a fifth of what they should have.

As they progressed through the bowl, random pieces of machinery started to hum softly, beginning to move and shift, changing in size and shape. Their perception skewed as the machines sped up their movement. Everything seemed to lose its sharp edges. Things seemed to blend together, flowing into, and around, one another. Simon saw his weapon's barrel twist like a live snake trying to escape his grip. Marco and Wendell seemed to flow into one being with dozens of small identical faces on the end of thin stalks, then the hand-shaped body broke in two, and re-formed back into Wendell and Marco once more.

The team struggled forward, starting up out of the bowl. Tripoli focused on the far arch, doing her best to ignore the wildly variable environment around them. Carter failed first. Tripoli turned as he tore his helmet off and howled madly, clawing at his armor as it seemed to liquefy and spin around him. He screamed like a lost child, falling to a fetal position and sublimating away.

Wendell died next, screaming and laughing like a madman as his auto-cannon spewed snow and fire. The cannon exploded, covering him in some liquid-like acid. He was still laughing as he melted away, his voice echoing faintly for some moments afterward.

Marco's armor collapsed as he seemed to deflate within it. The baggy armor and clothing struggled to hold its shape for a few seconds, then dropped flat on the ground, dissolving into a greenish mist that was slowly drawn into the whirling machinery.

Odd shapes and lights clattered, sped up, then gave a screech that drove ice shards into Tripoli's mind. Both her and Simon covered their ears, and struggled to stay upright, fighting for balance against the vertigo.

*Sarge is gone, I have to make it. I owe it to Sarge …*

Tripoli watched Simon pull himself painfully back together, and stumble a few steps more. Marco suddenly began to dissolve, then something ripped at her insides like broken glass. She gritted her teeth as her body tried to blow itself apart, holding her mind together through sheer stubbornness.

She took one step, then another, and another, staggering, barely upright as she fought forward. This was not about rescue any more. It was pure survival. She glanced to her right, and spotted Simon moving toward her. His movements were like an old man's, tentative and slow, fearful that he might fall apart with each step.

She raised her hand, gritting her teeth in pain. Simon's hand rose toward her. His face was skeletal, glistening threads of blood dripping from it. Their hands met, and Tripoli felt an electric charge tear through her. She dropped to her knees, gasping, still holding Simon's hand. His face was normal. His slightly off-center eyes gazed back at her in dazed recognition.

Simon got his feet under him, rising, his hand still wrapped around hers. She willed her legs to move. It was as if she hovered just outside of her body, unable to feel it, yet manipulating it, like pulling strings on a marionette.

They stumbled forward, then released each other's hands. Immediately, the wrenching feeling of being consumed returned. In his blind flailing, as he doubled over in pain, Simon struck Tripoli's arm. The sensation stopped as they made contact, leaving them both in a cold sweat inside their suits. Tripoli looked at Simon's grip on her arm, then at his face. He looked as shocky and pale as she felt, and guessed she didn't look any better to him. She wondered again if her suit had been compromised. If it was, then Simon's was also. She looked his suit over carefully for rips or punctures, and was relieved to find none.

"Come on, Private. Get your lazy ass up," she said with a pained gasp. "We got to finish this and get out. Command's got to know what happened."

She didn't wait for an answer, dragging the stocky medic to his feet. They both began to stumble through the machinery, slowly heading toward the bright aperture in the side of the mountain. Why they both thought this way was "out", wasn't questioned. It was the fastest way away from the painful, terrible machines.

The two of them staggered onward, toward the opening. Their steps became heavier, as if the world itself tried to crush them flat against it. Whimpering as they bogged down, Tripoli tried one last resort, and triggered her adrenalin dispenser. She felt the nozzle press against the large vein on her inner arm, and the high-pressure pump fired the concentrated liquid into her blood.

In moments, her heart rate tripled and everything slowed around her. The liquid had been added to the suits as a way to combat the shock of grievous wounds, giving a soldier a chance to survive, or spend their remaining life covering their team members. She reached over to her wrist comp, and triggered Simon's adrenalin pump remotely. Their steps steadied, though the terrible weight didn't recede. They reached the opening, and plunged through it. The light swallowed them whole.

Tripoli tightened her grip on his arm. She could barely make out the path through the blinding light. The path angled upwards suddenly, nearly causing them to lose their balance. She half-dragged him for-ward, covering front and left, as he tried to cover right and to the rear.

The light started to fade as they pushed on. Dim outlines that looked like large, twisted pillars that reminded Simon of the trees they'd first traveled through. His heart pounded from the adrenalin. Each footstep sounded like a gunshot, even muffled as they were through his helmet. His feet finally caught up with Tripoli's insistent tugging, and the two began to jog forward, double-timing their movement.

•     •     •

The ground began to crackle, like dry twigs rubbing against each other. Simon looked down, then focused his eyes forward, cold sweat forming anew across his brow as he realized they were jogging across bones. There were so many skeletons beneath them that the ground beneath them couldn't be seen.

The blue-green light vanished as they passed through a second archway. It opened into a clearing where the ground was bare rock with a translucent, brownish look to it. In the center of the clearing, lay the remains of six bodies. Simon knew who they were without looking at the ID tags. He knew the bulky outlines of Wendell and Carter. He recognized Vinson's lanky form lying next to Marco. There two more, their hands clasped together: himself, and Tripoli.

Tripoli dropped to the ground next to her own body. The adrenalin was wearing off, leaving her completely exhausted, unable to react to the scene in front of her. She was too tired to scream.

Simon collapsed next to her as his own adrenalin stimulation wore off. He kept staring at the two bodies with their hands intertwined.

"That's ... us?" he asked Tripoli.

"I don't know," she replied tiredly, then her voice hardened. "No, that's not us. It's just an illusion this crappy place is doing to us. It's like the stupid illusions before we went full seal! They're not real!"

She lurched to her feet, and screamed in incoherent rage. "THEY. ARE. NOT. REAL!"

The plant roots shot from the ground, entangling them both. Tripoli was pulled under, struggling against their grip, still screaming. The plants arrowed toward Simon, then seemed to pause, as if waiting. He stared back, fear gnawing his stomach raw.

"I ... I'm ...", he started, then began to cough, sobbing raggedly. "I didn't want to die ... I didn't ... I ... oh god ..."

The plants ignored him, drawing back down into the ground. The clearing faded as another arch appeared.

"I didn't wanna die," he sobbed as his feet impelled him through the grey gate, then he disappeared.

Tripoli watched him fade, and a raw scream of rage and despair ripped from her throat as the vines finished dragging her into the ground.  Her vision faded to black ...

●　　　●　　　●

The hatchway door swung open, slamming with a hollow clang against the bulkhead. The lanky Sergeant Vinson in full combat gear woke the team. His raspy drawl sounded like a bandsaw cutting metal.

"Y'all be gettin' up! Control's got us'ns a mission ta go! Report fer briefin' in five!"

"Yes, Sergeant!"

The five-unit team shouted as they scrambled out of their bunks, and stumbled to their lockers.

Corporal Tripoli watched the others beginning their daily kit up. Grabbing the door of her locker, she lifted its latch. She paused and looked at her hand. There had been the faintest sensation that someone's hand had held hers for a moment. Turning away from her locker, she looked at the rest of the team, then shrugged.

She finished kitting up, then pulled her helmet out of her locker, hanging it on a belt loop before hurrying after the others to the briefing.

# ABOUT THE AUTHOR

J Dark is a latecomer to the writing profession, but enjoying every moment that life will allow. "The best thing to me is writing a story that someone enjoys. If I've made something fun and entertaining for people, it's a win-win."

The author lives with a house full of dreams, three cats, and various friends who occasionally drop by and stay for a while. The author lives in Kansas, where the winds blow all the time, and, if you blink your eyes, the weather changes.

J Dark is the author of the "Glass Bottles" series and the short story collection, *Sometimes After Dark.* You can find out more about their work at *The Pandemonium* (*thepandemonium.net*).

# You Might Also Enjoy

## BEST SERVED COLD

by Bob Schoonover

*A dish of corporate greed served with a side of revenge.*

## PARRISH BLUE

by Vanessa MacLaren-Wray

*Sallie never expected to discover a world she'd forgotten how to imagine.*

## REDUCTION IN FORCE

by Steve Soult

*A heartless corporate layoff leaves Gil Schaffer emotionally shattered.*

Available in digital and trade paperback editions from
Water Dragon Publishing
*waterdragonpublishing.com*